JIM NASIUM

STONE ARCH BOOKS
a capstone imprint

Jim Nasium
is published by Stone Arch Books,
a Capstone Imprint
1710 Roe Crest Drive
North Mankato, Minnesota 56003
www.capstoneyoungreaders.com

Cataloging-in-Publication Data is available on
the Library of Congress website.
ISBN: 978-1-4965-3026-4 (reinforced library bound)
ISBN: 978-1-4965-3028-8 (paperback)
ISBN: 978-1-4965-3030-1 (eBook pdf)

Summary: Jim Nasium is desperate to live up to his name and find
the perfect sport to suit his yet-to-be-discovered skills! This time Jim
tries his luck on the tennis court. With the help of his friend, Milo,
and poetry teacher, Mr. Donaldson, Jim makes improvements in his
game. But will the coach's plan to pair Jim and his dreamgirl on a
mixed doubles team be a double fault?

Printed and bound in the United States of America.
009623F16

JIM NASIUM

Is a Tennis Mismatch

WRITTEN BY
MARTY MCKNIGHT

ILLUSTRATED BY
CHRIS JONES

CONTENTS

CHAPTER ONE

LOVE-LOVE AT FIRST SIGHT

"Game point!" I twirled my table tennis paddle.

At the other end of the green table stood — wobbled might be a better word, actually — my best friend, Milo Cabrera.

"You do realize," I said with a smug smile, "that I'm just one point away from winning?"

Milo pushed his glasses up his nose, which was dripping with sweat. "Yeah, yeah," he said. "Just get it over with."

Around us, the flashing lights and dinging bells of the FUN! Zone . . . well, flashed and dinged. At the air hockey table, two ponytailed girls smashed a plinking puck back and forth. A trio of teens rolled Skee-balls up ramps. A sweaty grown-up danced his heart out to a video game called *All the Right Moves*.

It was a busy afternoon, and the place was hopping. It helped that the FUN! Zone was right near our school, Bennett City Elementary. *Go Buffaloes!*

THWACK!

I served, and the ping pong ball zinged perfectly to Milo's side. He wound up, stuck out his tongue in concentration, and —

WHIFF!

"That's game!" I said.

Milo shook his head. "Where'd you learn to play like that?" he asked.

"There's a table at my uncle Dave's house," I said.

"Dang," he said. "How often do you visit?"

I ignored him. "Rematch?"

Milo served first. The ball came over the net.

I swung my paddle in a wide arc, blasting a backhand with wicked topspin out of Milo's reach.

Two girls strolled up to the table. I recognized Amy Choo but not the other girl. "Nice backhand," she said as they breezed past.

"Huh?" I said. Girls rarely spoke to me.

Milo took advantage of my distraction by serving before I was ready. In his hurry, he crushed the ball so hard that it didn't even hit the table.

PING!

The ball ricocheted off my forehead.

"Ow!" I rubbed the stinging spot.

"Sorry," Milo said.

"Who was she?"

Milo pointed with his paddle. "That's Olivia Hartford. Her first day at our school is tomorrow. I hear she's a star tennis player. Coach Pittman's been really excited about Olivia transferring to Bennett City."

The girls looked over at us from the popcorn machine, and Olivia smiled at me. Like, actually smiled.

A brilliant idea tripped into my brain.

"You know, Milo," I said, "I've been thinking. Maybe I should join the school tennis team."

Milo shook his head, which made his glasses slip down his nose again. "Jim Nasium, that ball you took to the head has affected your powers of logic."

* * *

Yeah, you heard him right. The name's Jim Nasium — don't wear it out!

With a name like mine, I should be a sports sensation. You know, a real gym class hero!

The problem is . . . I lack some serious game.

You've heard that old saying, "born with two left feet." Well, I was born with two left feet AND two left arms!

That's a real problem in tennis — or any sport, for that matter. And I'd know. At this point, I've tried just about every sport on the planet.

The result? Well, let's just say I've warmed some very nice benches in my day.

But this time is going to be different.

This time, I won't be a tennis mismatch. I'll be a tennis ace!

CHAPTER TWO

CLASS CLOWN

"Love is in the air!"

Mr. Donaldson stood before our class. He placed his hands over his heart. "Love *sonnets*, that is. A sonnet is a fourteen-line poem about a specific idea or feeling, like falling in love."

Behind me, Bobby Studwell groaned. Bobby was forever the thorn in my side, the lump of coal in my stocking, the corn kernel stuck in my teeth.

"Here's one of my favorites." Mr. Donaldson cleared his throat. "How do I love thee? Let me count the ways — "

KNOCK KNOCK!

"Saved by the bell," Bobby said.

I didn't bother correcting his cliché.

Mr. Donaldson opened the door, and there she stood. Tall. Strawberry-blonde hair. A constellation of freckles across her nose and cheeks.

Olivia Hartford.

"Ah!" Mr. Donaldson chirped. "Our new student has arrived! Come in!"

Olivia clutched a notebook and scanned the room for an empty desk.

"There's a seat over here!" Bobby Studwell said from behind me. He tried to sound nice, but I wasn't buying it.

"Thanks," Olivia said, sitting in the open desk between Bobby and his henchman, Tommy Strong.

"Olivia, would you like to share a little info about yourself with the class?" Mr. Donaldson asked.

Olivia stood back up. She brushed a stray piece of hair behind her ear. "Well," she said. "My name's Olivia Hartford. I like playing tennis and reading books, and my favorite food is strawberry ice cream." She shrugged. "That's . . . um . . . me."

"Welcome to Bennett City Elementary, Miss Hartford," Mr. Donaldson said.

"Go Buffaloes!" Bobby and Tommy said, thumping their fists on their desks.

Milo raised his hand.

"Yes, Milo?" Mr. Donaldson asked.

"Olivia, do you know why fish don't make good tennis players?" Milo asked.

She looked confused. "Uh, no."

Milo beamed. "Because they always get caught in the net."

HA HA HA HA HA!

The class erupted in laughter. Even Mr. Donaldson smiled as he shushed us.

"Thank you, Miss Hartford," he said.

Olivia sat back down.

"Now, I'd like one of you students to give Miss Hartford a tour of our fine school today," he continued. "Make her feel at home. Do I have any volunteers?"

This is my chance! I thought.

I looked at Milo. He knew what I was thinking. He gave me a nod and a thumbs-up.

My hand shot into the air.

"Jim Nasium!" Mr. Donaldson said. "Would you like to volunteer?"

I glanced at Olivia . . . and froze.

"Mr. Nasium?"

"I . . . I . . . I need to go to the bathroom!" I blurted out. "May I?"

I panicked.

"Of course," Mr. Donaldson said. He held out the hall pass.

I grabbed the pass and headed to the door. I was too embarrassed to look at Olivia.

Behind me, I heard Bobby Studwell say, "I'll volunteer!"

"Thank you, Mr. Studwell," Mr. Donaldson said.

Just my luck.

In the hall, I tried to gather my nerves. How was I ever going to show Olivia what a great guy I was if I couldn't even be around her?

And then I saw it.

There on the wall. Right next to a poster for the upcoming *SPRING FLING!* school dance was a bulletin board with a sign-up sheet for the tennis team.

I strode over to the bulletin board. I used a pencil dangling from a string to scribble my name.

CHAPTER THREE

COURT JESTER

The Bennett City Elementary tennis team met at the courts outside the school. I had my dad's old tennis racket. It was wooden, and there were two strings missing.

Olivia Hartford stood nearby. A pink headband held her hair back, highlighting eyes as green as a pair of leprechaun boots.

I imagined my own eyes turning into giant red hearts, like in a cartoon or an emoji.

"What are you doing here, Nasium?" Bobby Studwell snorted. "Run out of benches to warm?"

I didn't know when I'd joined the team that Bobby was on it. *Just my luck. AGAIN.*

"All right, everyone! Line up!" yelled Coach Pittman. No, not *that* Coach Pittman. This was Coach *Annette* Pittman, the other Coach Pittman's twin sister. Did you follow that? Anyway, she was just as tall and muscular as her twin brother.

And she was just as intimidating.

I stood on the white-striped baseline with the other boys and girls and tried to look like I knew what I was doing.

And then Milo showed up.

"Sorry I'm late!" he shouted as he ran in.

Milo was wearing short white shorts with red-striped knee-high socks, a white shirt, and thick sweatbands on his head and wrists. He looked . . . interesting.

"Please continue," Milo said, lining up next to me. "I really didn't mean to cause . . . *a racket.*"

HA HA HA HA HA!

Coach Pittman blew her whistle. "We're gonna have a great season. I see a lot of new faces, including last year's All-State Junior Tennis Champion, Olivia Hartford!"

Olivia waved her racket.

"Now," Coach Pittman said, "I'm going split you into pairs so you can hit with your partner as a warm-up!" She pointed to random players, assigning them together. "Jim Nasium and . . . "

Please say Milo. Please say Milo. Please say—

"Olivia!"

I almost Bjorned in my Borgs.

Say it with me: *Just. My. Luck.*

Olivia and I walked together to one of the five tennis courts lined up side by side. Milo was three courts away from us. He was teamed up with Amy Choo.

Olivia bounced a tennis ball. "Let's see what you've got, Jim," she said with a smile.

COUGH! COUGH!

I couldn't even form words.

Olivia tossed the ball high and served a sizzling shot that zipped past me.

From the court beside us, Bobby laughed. Olivia pulled a second tennis ball from her pocket. "You'll get it this time," she said.

THWACK!

Olivia's second serve was faster than her first. It shot between my legs, making me leap into the air.

This is NOT going well, I thought.

Olivia produced a third ball. "This one's got your name on it," she said.

THWACK!

Another sizzler came rocketing toward me. I was determined to hit it as hard as I could. I wound up and swung.

WHIFF!

I missed, which would have been bad enough, but I also kinda lost my grip on my racket. It sailed through the air and whizzed over the net. When it finally returned to the earth, its handle broke off before it clattered to a stop.

Right at Olivia's feet.

Olivia looked down at my broken racket with wide, shocked eyes.

My cheeks burned red.

"Smile and wave, Nasium," Bobby chortled from the next court.

My heart was as fractured as my crummy old tennis racket.

CHAPTER FOUR

POETRY IN MOTION

RUFF! RUFF! RUFF!

I heard Tank before I saw him.

Milo's bulldog was a lumbering beast that lived up to his name. He trampled up the hill toward the Bennett City Park tennis courts where I waited. Slobber flew from his jowls, and the ground trembled as he bounded.

Milo came jogging after him. He wore the same outrageous tennis outfit as he had at practice. Only now he'd added a baby-blue sweater that was tied around his neck. He had also pinned a golden tennis racket-shaped charm to his lapel.

"Wait up, Tank!" Milo hollered.

Tank didn't wait up. He plowed me over.

"OOF!"

I dropped the new tennis racket I'd bought at Al's Sporting Goods, and I landed in the grass. I couldn't help but laugh as Tank licked my face and arms. It wasn't the first time he'd knocked me to the ground.

"At least *you* love me," I said, scratching him behind one ear. "Even if you do have terrible breath."

"Ready to practice?" Milo asked.

"Yep." I stood, picking up my racket.

"Good. I hired us a tutor. He should be here any second."

Milo had a backpack over one shoulder. He unzipped and upended it. Tennis balls poured out. They were dirty and covered in bite marks.

"Sorry," he said. "Tank's low on chew toys."

Tank snatched a tennis ball up into his slobbery jaws and gnawed on it.

Just then, a voice I totally recognized shouted, "Jim! Milo! So wonderful to see you!"

Mr. Donaldson came strolling up to the court. He wore large sunglasses, a red T-shirt with matching plaid shorts, and a floppy hat more commonly seen on fishermen.

"Mr. Donaldson," Milo said. "I like your style."

"Right back at you, Milo," Mr. Donaldson said. "I'm very excited you asked me to help you. Back in my day, I was quite the tennis player." He swung his racket in a graceful forehand loop. "Still am, if I do say so myself."

We started our lesson by dropping our rackets to the court.

"Tennis is a dance," Mr. Donaldson explained. "It's a love sonnet between you and the court. It's poetry in motion. Follow my lead."

He swayed in one direction, flailing his arms out and swinging them around. He danced from one side of the court to the other.

Milo looked at me and shrugged. "Why not?"

I felt ridiculous, but did it anyway. I waved my arms from side to side, dancing around like the world's worst ballerina.

Tank watched us curiously. He barked from time to time, probably because he just wanted the whole thing to end.

Finally, Mr. Donaldson stopped. "Rackets up!" he shouted.

We grabbed our rackets and held them aloft.

"Now, each move that I just showed you corresponds with a tennis swing," he said. He then described a bunch of different ways to grip a tennis racket. Apparently that's important. Who knew!? Well, Mr. Donaldson did. He showed us the Eastern Grip, which is important for forehands. The Continental Grip — good for serving.

And one called the Western Grip, which felt super awkward to me.

"I'm never gonna remember these," Milo said. "Unless there's a Video Game Controller grip. *That* I'd remember."

"Come on, boys!" Mr. Donaldson said. "Let's try it out!"

He lined up on the other side of the net and then bopped the ball to me with his racket. It lazily bounced once before I swatted it back to him.

"There you go!" Mr. Donaldson said. "Huzzah!"

"Sure, I'm awesome if we play in slow motion," I said.

"Then let's pick up the speed."

Mr. Donaldson's second hit zipped across the net.

I unleashed a mighty two-handed backhand.

THWACK!

The tennis ball sailed through the air far above Mr. Donaldson's head and flew over the tennis court's fence.

"Crikey," Milo said, adjusting his sweater. "I wish you'd known about the Western Grip before baseball season."

"Me, too," I said.

"Tank!" Milo shouted. "Fetch!"

RUFF! RUFF!

Tank happily chased after the ball.

"Not so hard this time," Mr. Donaldson said. "Remember to be light on your feet, Jim, my boy. Graceful." He danced a little jig and then served.

I sent it sailing over his head. Again.

Milo seemed to get the hang of it pretty quick. "It's because I'm a better dancer than you," he claimed.

I, however, kept Tank busy for the next hour. I hit the ball left, right, up, and over. Pretty much anywhere but in bounds. Tank was getting quite a workout, fetching all of my crazy hits.

Finally, Mr. Donaldson said, "One more." The ball in his hand was coated in Tank spit.

A spray of drool flew off the ball when he hit it. It corkscrewed over the net.

I swung a nice, level forehand stroke and struck the ball perfectly.

SPLAT!

When the wet ball met my racket, spittle shot through the strings.

It sprayed my face and arms.

"Perfect!" Mr. Donaldson chirruped. "Just inside the line. Well done, Jim!"

"Really?" I said.

I hadn't seen my shot land. I was too busy wiping doggie drool off my face.

Tank wobbled over and plucked the ball off the court.

PLOP!

He spit the chewed-up tennis ball coated with bulldog slobber into my waiting palm.

"Ugh," I said. "Good boy."

CHAPTER FIVE:

DOUBLES DATE

"All right," Coach Pittman said. "I'm going to mix things up a bit."

"Must be an old family saying," I said under my breath. Coach Pittman's brother, the *other* Coach Pittman, loved saying the same thing. And it usually meant I was about to be placed in a tight spot.

So I braced myself.

"Olivia, based on what I've seen in practice, I'm giving you a new doubles partner," Coach Pittman said.

Yeah, I won't even finish what she said. You know who she picked.

Olivia nodded. "Got it, Coach," she said, like it didn't even faze her that she'd just been paired with the worst player on the team. "Come on, Jim."

I followed Olivia to our court, watching her pigtails sway like two beautiful metronomes keeping the beat of my heart. My racket trembled in my hands. The Eagles players on the other side of the net eyed us hungrily.

Olivia pulled me so close that I could smell her bubble gum lip gloss. "Just follow my lead," she said.

"Bahhhhhhh," I answered. I still couldn't form words around Olivia.

It was our serve first.

Olivia prepared to serve. "Let's do this, Jim," she said. "Love-love."

"Okay . . . " I managed to squeak out, "honey-bunny?"

Olivia's face scrunched up. "Um, that's the score, Jim," she said. "It's zero-zero. In tennis, we say love-love."

"I . . . oh," I said. I really wished I could just jetpack out of there.

I took my place on the opposite side of the centerline as Olivia, up near the net. She tossed the ball high and smashed a serve at the Eagles. Their back player boomed a forehand shot across the net, right past me.

"Whoa!" I shouted as Olivia sent it back over the net with a ripping backhand.

The Eagles lobbed it high into the air. It arced toward me.

This is my chance!

I danced to the perfect spot and waited. I swung.

THWACK!

Like a fish playing tennis, my shot got caught in the net.

Great, I thought. *Mr. Donaldson's dance moves and grip lesson didn't work.*

The next few points, Olivia raced around the court while I tried to stay clear of the ball. I may or may not have been standing out of bounds. But we won the first game, and we won the second, too, thanks to Olivia.

When it was my turn to serve, I either pounded the ball into the net or over the Eagle players' heads. One of my shots zipped past Olivia's ear so close it made her pigtail fly up.

The match was close, but when it was over, we'd miraculously won. Well, Olivia won. And I got to stand sort of close to her.

CHAPTER SIX

A NEW HOPE

Everyone at school was talking about the Spring Fling dance. Posters all over the halls said things like: *Shake Your Buffalo Backsides!* Student passed notes about it in class, during lunch, and from the top of the monkey bars during recess. It was one of those formal dances, the kind where you have to dress up in suits and skirts and bring a date.

And I was going to ask Olivia Hartford to go with me.

Yeah, I know. Even after my terrible performance at the tennis meet.

"Olivia," I began, my voice trembling. "Will you go to the Spring Fling Dance with me?"

"*Of course, Jim, my love!*" Milo said with a high voice, pretending to be Olivia. "See? That was easy, wasn't it?"

Milo and I stood by my locker. I could still barely form words around Olivia, so I wanted to practice what I was going to *try* to say with Milo beforehand. Olivia was down the hall, clustered near Amy Choo's locker with two other girls.

I cupped my hand over my mouth and nose and exhaled. "Yikes," I said. "Cafeteria breath. Do you have a mint?"

Milo dug through his pocket and pulled out a box of mints. I chewed through a good handful of them.

"You can do it, Jim," Milo said, like a boxing coach in my corner.

I wished I had the same confidence.

Still, I found a way to put one foot in front of the other. With each step, my courage grew. I was making my way toward her. I was going to do it! I was going to—

THUD!

Bobby Studwell slammed into me. I dropped my books as he beelined past.

"Hi, Bobby," Olivia said.

I knelt down to scoop up my scattered books.

"Great match the other day," he said to Olivia. "You know, even though Nasium was your partner and almost ruined it." He glanced over at me picking up my books and smirked.

"Thanks," Olivia said. She looked over at me, too, just as I was standing back up. "I think Jim has a lot of potential, though."

I dropped my books again.

"Ha!" Bobby said. "Good one, Olivia." He stopped to scratch behind his head. "Say, I was wondering if you had a date for the Spring Fling."

"Oh," Olivia said. "Uh, I . . . I don't."

Amy Choo and the other girls scattered, leaving Olivia and Bobby alone. Well, alone except for the guy peeling his books off the floor for the second time.

"Wanna go with me?" Bobby asked.

"Oh." Olivia was taken aback. "Thanks, but . . . well, Amy and some of the other girls are all going together. No dates."

"No dates?" Bobby sounded confused.

It's his default emotion.

"I'll see you there, though," she said.

Watching her turn him down was almost as delicious as an ice cold Cherry Mega-Slurp. As Bobby turned away, his shoulders slumped.

Olivia said, "Even though I won't have a date, it doesn't mean I'm not saving a dance for someone special."

When she said it, Bobby and I were standing right next to each other. Bobby and I looked at each other and then at Olivia. Olivia spun on one delicate, perfect foot and hurried off to rejoin her friends.

"She was talkin' to me, Double Fault," Bobby said, nudging my books, which cascaded floorward. He laughed and left.

She was looking at me! I thought. I gathered my books, hugging them to my chest. *She was talking to me!*

"Dude!" Milo ran up to me. "You didn't ask her."

I sighed. "I didn't need to. She's saving me a dance."

A wide grin spread across Milo's face. "She is? Way to go, Jim!"

He clapped me hard on the back, and my stack of books crashed to the floor for a fourth time.

This time, though, I didn't care. Not. One. Single. Bit.

CHAPTER SEVEN:

A FORMAL DISASTER

"Oh, you two look so handsome!"

My mom stood with her camera ready as I walked into the living room the night of the Spring Fling. I had on one of my dad's old, rumpled suits and a bow tie. Milo also wore a suit, only his was bright blue. A pair of gold tennis ball cufflinks gleamed from each of his wrists.

"Are you both excited for the dance?" my mom asked as she snapped a photo.

"Totally!" Milo said, happily adjusting his cufflinks.

I thought of Olivia Hartford and me dancing together to the world's loveliest love song and added, "More than words can express."

The Spring Fling was in full swing by the time we arrived.

Balloons and streamers filled the school gymnasium. A fake waterfall made out of glitter and cardboard twinkled along one wall of bleachers. A DJ on a platform spun tracks under one of the basketball hoops.

Coach Pittman and Coach Pittman guarded the snack table and punch bowl. Milo went right for it, piling high a plate with popcorn, crackers, and cheese.

"How's the tennis team going, Jim?" asked Coach Pittman, the male version.

"Fine, I guess," I said.

"He's got a great doubles partner," said Coach Pittman, the female version.

"Olivia Hartford?" asked Coach Pittman #1.

"If anyone can unlock Jim's potential, it's her," said Coach Pittman #2.

Yeah, I added to myself, *if I can ever be around her without acting like a fool.*

Speaking of Olivia, I spied her on the dance floor. She wore a pink dress and tennis shoes. Her hair was not in pigtails. Instead, it spun around her face like a gilded frame containing a priceless work of art.

I almost fainted into the punch bowl.

Olivia and Amy Choo danced with their girl group. Nearby, Bobby Studwell and Tommy Strong scarfed down food.

"Come on," Milo said. He waved his arms over his head. "Let's dance!"

Milo dragged me by the arm out onto the dancefloor.

He pretended to act like a robot, then spun around like a top, then wriggled like a worm. Soon enough, I was dancing alongside him. We looked like two broken water sprinklers. Or two bus drivers whose legs had fallen asleep. Or two guys mowing lawn.

HA HA HA HA HA!

Bobby and Tommy laughed at us.

"Nice dancing, Nasium!" Bobby said.

My ears burned red. I glanced at Olivia, and she was looking right at me.

"You're about as graceful on the dance floor as you are on the tennis court!" Tommy said.

Bobby waved his empty paper plate like a tennis racket. Then he took some cheese slices off Tommy's plate, wadded them together, and tossed the cheese ball into the air.

"Tennis Champ serving Court Dork!" he shouted. "Match point!"

He swung the paper plate.

SMACK!

The cheeseball flew across the dance floor and headed right at me.

SPLAT!

The wad of cheese hit me right in the chest. It rolled down my dad's suit coat and schlorped onto the floor.

HA HA HA HA HA!

Bobby and Tommy roared with glee.

Olivia stared at me like I was a wounded animal.

I wove my way through the gym, heading for the door, Milo following.

CHAPTER EIGHT:

IN THE ZONE

Even though I wasn't in the mood for fun, Milo convinced me to go to the FUN! Zone. It was a pretty quiet night. Most of the kids were at the Spring Fling.

We went straight for the ping pong table. I slipped out of my cheesy suitcoat.

"Maybe I should quit the team," I said. "I mean, I can't even defend myself from Cheddar." I served to Milo.

WHIFF!

Milo missed.

"I only joined because of Olivia," I continued, putting sidespin on the ball.

WHIFF!

"There are tons of players who'd be a better doubles partner than me." I uncorked a topspin serve at Milo.

WHIFF!

Milo threw down his paddle. "Jim!" he said. "Do you realize you're winning without even trying?"

I looked at my paddle. I looked at the ball. I looked at Milo.

"You're overthinking things," said Milo. "Talking to Olivia. Playing tennis. You're letting your head get in the way."

I scratched my noggin.

"Can I play the winner?" said a voice behind me.

I spun around. Olivia had one hand on her hip. The other held a ping pong paddle. Amy Choo was with her.

"Uhhhhhhhh," I said.

"Jim!" Milo hissed. He pointed at his head.

Right, I thought. *Just say something! Don't overthink it.* "Sure!" I blurted out. "I'm really good at ping pong."

"You sound so confident," Olivia said. "Bring it on."

Olivia sidled up to Milo's side of the table. A look of determination filled her eyes.

"Love-love," I said.

"Okay, honey-bunny," Olivia joked.

I served first, sending a wicked burner across the table.

THWACK!

Olivia fired it right back at me. I was used to playing against Milo, so her shot caught me off-guard.

THWACK!

I sent it back to her.

We volleyed until Olivia finally snuck a shot past me.

"Point!" she cried, raising her paddle.

She was good, and I didn't care that I was getting my Buffalo backside kicked. I was playing table tennis with a pretty girl.

Then Amy and Milo jumped in to play doubles against Olivia and me. After just a couple laid-back volleys, it was like something clicked. Olivia and I moved in-sync with each other, like we'd been doing it forever.

Turns out, I got that dance with Olivia after all.

CHAPTER NINE

A MATCH MADE IN HEAVEN?

After Olivia and I broke the ice on the ping pong table, I found myself able to string together sentences when talking to her at practice. We picked up right where we'd left off at the FUN! Zone.

During one practice, Coach Pittman called us over. "Hartford and Nasium," she said, "I've noticed that you make a great team. So in our next match, you'll be taking on the Rattlesnakes' strongest doubles team, Katie and Kelly King."

GULP!

I tried to speak, but there was a lump the size of a tennis ball in my throat.

"The King Sisters?" Olivia's face turned white as a ghost. "They're the best tennis players in the state!"

"Wait, I thought *you* were the best tennis player in the state," I said.

"My record is 35-1," Olivia said. "And I'll give you zero guesses to figure out who handed me that one loss."

The look of fear in Olivia's eyes spiked those little hairs on the back of my neck.

We were gonna need to bring our A-game if we wanted to stand a chance.

Later that practice, Olivia and I scrimmaged against Bobby Studwell and Tommy Strong. We had them flailing around like two fish caught in a net. At one point, Olivia hit an overhead smash at Bobby so fast, he dove out of the way.

WHACK!

He bellyflopped on the court with a loud, **"OOF!"**

The ball landed inbounds. Olivia and I slapped high-five.

"That's what you get for hurling cheese at my partner!" Olivia shouted, shaking her beautiful fist.

CHAPTER TEN

SMASHING SUCCESS

The day of the tennis meet, I showed up ready to play. I had my headband and wristbands on and my shoes tied tight. I was determined to win. I wasn't going to let the King Sisters get the best of us.

And then I saw them.

"I wanna go home," I said, turning to flee.

Milo grabbed me by the collar. "You'll be fine, Jim," he said.

"Easy for you to say," I muttered.

Katie and Kelly King were tall and powerful. They moved like two cyborgs created in a sports laboratory with the specific purpose of crushing tennis balls . . . and other tennis players' souls.

Whatever mojo Olivia and I had built at practice, the King Sisters made it disappear. They hit everything we sent their way: forehands, backhands, overhead smashes. Didn't matter.

We lost the first set, 6-3. The King Sisters didn't let up a bit in the second set. We were quickly down 3-1.

It was Olivia's serve, and I could see she was upset. I jogged to the baseline, and we huddled together.

"We're getting destroyed," Olivia said. "I don't think we can win, Jim."

Olivia was overthinking. I was determined not to give up, and I had an idea. "Olivia," I said, "If we want to win this, we have to do what I do best."

"What's that?" Olivia asked.

"We dance!" I struck a pose, just like Mr. Donaldson showed me.

Olivia began to laugh. When she finished, we took a couple deep breaths. The next time the Kings served, Olivia and I moved like we did at the ping pong table. We rallied back to win the second set 6-4.

"Way to go, guys!" Milo cheered from the sidelines. A giant, floppy hat was perched atop his head to go with the rest of his wild wardrobe. Mr. Donaldson sat next to him wearing an almost identical outfit and giving me a thumbs-up. In fact, the whole team had stopped by to watch us.

The final set was a real battle. Each team won four games before Olivia and I surged ahead, 5-4.

The score was 40-40, or deuce. Olivia served the ball as hard as she could.

The King Sisters were ready. Katie sent a forehand shot right back at Olivia.

Olivia stepped left and then swung.

THWACK!

Her shot went deep across the court toward the white baseline. Katie King chased after it but didn't swing. She thought it was going to be out of bounds.

The ball hit the line and skipped out of reach.

Kelly King groaned.

"Advantage, us!" Olivia said, pumping her fist. "Match point, Jim!"

We were just a single point away from winning!

The King Sisters grumbled and gripped their rackets tighter. If they truly were cyborgs, lasers would have been shooting out of their eyes at us.

Olivia served, and Kelly King sent it right back. My head whipped side to side as I watched the blurry yellow ball zip back and forth across the net. Olivia moved faster than I'd ever seen before.

Finally, Katie King sent a shot right at the back corner of our court. Olivia raced after it. The only shot she had was a looping backhand that sent the ball high into the air.

It was just what the Kings wanted.

SMASH!

Katie King hit the ball so hard that I thought the fuzzy cover would come flying off. The ball scorched the air around it.

I jumped left — right in front of the oncoming shot. All I could do was toss up my racket and hope for the best.

THWACK!

The ball hit my racket, which ricocheted back and nailed me in the forehead. I fell to the court.

From the ground, I saw the ball fly away and hit the top of the net.

No! I thought.

The ball teetered . . . then it dropped.

Right onto the King Sisters' side of the court! There was no way to hit it back.

Katie and Kelly King dropped their rackets to the court in despair.

The court swarmed with Buffaloes. Olivia helped me to my feet.

"Nice match, love-love," she said. Then she planted a kiss right on my cheek.

I fainted.

When I came to, Milo helped me back to my feet the second time. "Is anyone else hungry?" he asked.

The team looked puzzled. Me especially.

"Because I could eat some waffles," Milo said. He pointed at my face.

HA HA HA HA HA!

The team laughed.

"I don't get it," I said.

Coach Pittman stepped close and leaned down until I could see my reflection in her sunglasses.

The crisscrossing strings on my racket had left a waffle-like impression on my forehead.

"Just keep the syrup out of my hair," I said.

HA HA HA HA HA!

AUTHOR

Marty McKnight is a freelance writer from St. Paul, Minnesota. He once defeated his dog, 6-0, 6-1, in a grueling tennis match. He has written many chapter books for young readers.

ILLUSTRATOR

Chris Jones is a children's illustrator based in Canada. He has worked as both a graphic designer and an illustrator. His illustrations have appeared in several magazines and educational publications, and he also has numerous graphic novels and children's books to his credit. Chris is inspired by good music, books, long walks, and generous amounts of coffee.

CHECK OUT ALL

JIM NASIUM

SPORT ADVENTURES

JIM NASIUM Is A Football Fumbler
BY MARTY McKNIGHT & CHRIS JONES

JIM NASIUM Is A Basket Case
BY MARTY McKNIGHT & CHRIS JONES

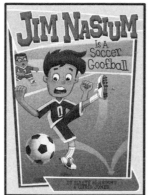

JIM NASIUM Is A Soccer Goofball
BY MARTY McKNIGHT & CHRIS JONES

JIM NASIUM Is A Hockey Hazard
BY MARTY McKNIGHT & CHRIS JONES

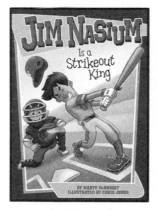

JIM NASIUM Is a Strikeout King
BY MARTY McKNIGHT ILLUSTRATED BY CHRIS JONES

JIM NASIUM Is a Tennis Mismatch
BY MARTY McKNIGHT ILLUSTRATED BY CHRIS JONES